One, Two ... Where's the Shoe?

Story by Richard Rosenstein
Illustrated by Victor Ambrus

Floris Books

Mr and Mrs Shoemaker had ten children.

All day long the children played. When evening came, they took off their shoes and lined them up in a neat row outside the house before snuggling into bed.

Then their father or mother would count the pairs of shoes to make sure that nobody was missing.

One evening Mr Shoemaker was out counting the pairs of shoes: "One, two, three, four, five, six, seven, eight, nine ... nine pairs of shoes!"

"Where is the last pair?" he wondered. He called inside to his wife: "One of the children is missing! There are only nine pairs of shoes here."

"Nonsense!" came a voice from the house. Mrs Shoemaker came out and began to count: "One, two, three, four, five, six, seven, eight, nine ... nine pairs of shoes!"

"Oh dear," she said, "where is the last one?"
So she called indoors: "José, one of the children is missing!
There are only nine pairs of shoes here."

"Are you sure?" a voice replied. Out came José, a friend from Spain, and started to count: "Uno, dos, tres, cuatro, cinco, seis, siete, ocho, nueve ... nine pairs of shoes!"

"You're quite right. Where could the child be?"
So he called Giovanni, the gardener.
"Giovanni, one of the children is missing! There are only
nine pairs of shoes here."

"They were all here a while ago," said Giovanni, who came from Italy. "Let me see," and he too started to count:

"Uno, due, tre, quattro, cinque, sei, sette, otto, nove ... nine pairs of shoes!"

"That's very strange," he said. So he called over to Maria, the neighbour's daughter. "Maria, one of the children is missing! There are only nine pairs of shoes tonight."

"You can't have counted properly," said Maria. "I saw all the children take their shoes off just now."

So Maria came out and started to count as well — in German as she came from Germany:

"Eins, zwei, drei, vier, fünf, sechs, sieben, acht, neun ... nine pairs of shoes!"

"Oh," she said, "I could have sworn I saw all the children here just now." So she called Mr Jeannot, the new French teacher, who was cycling down the road.

"Monsieur Jeannot, one of the children is missing! There are only nine pairs of shoes tonight."

"Oh really!" said Monsieur Jeannot, getting off his bicycle laden with books and vegetables and he started to count — in French, of course:

"Un, deux, trois, quatre, cinq, six, sept, huit, neuf ... nine pairs of shoes!"

"Ah, indeed, there is a pair missing."

"What shall we do?" cried Mrs Shoemaker, looking very worried.

Just then the door opened and out rushed Joanna, the youngest daughter.

"Look! Look! Johnny has gone to bed with his shoes on!"
Mr and Mrs Shoemaker looked at one another with
surprise. They all went inside to see little Johnny snoring
away with his shoes sticking out from underneath the
blanket.